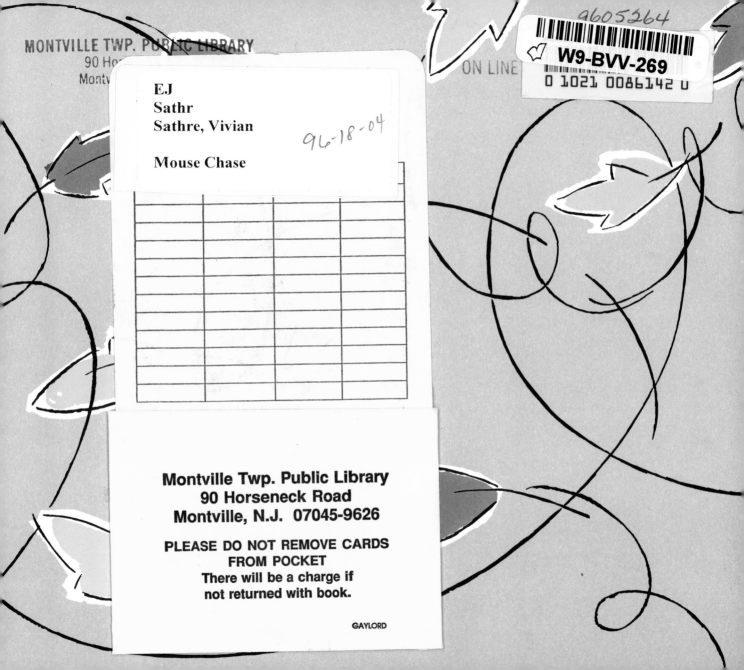

Mouse Chase

Written by **Vivian Sathre**

Illustrated by **Ward Schumaker**

Harcourt Brace & Company

San Diego   New York   London

Requests for permission to make copies of any part of the work should be mailed to:
Permissions Department, Harcourt Brace & Company,
6277 Sea Harbor Drive, Orlando, Florida 32887-6777.

Library of Congress Cataloging-in-Publication Data
Sathre, Vivian.
Mouse chase/Vivian Sathre;
illustrated by Ward Schumaker.—1st ed.
p.   cm
Summary: A mouse escapes the clutches of a
cat by riding on a windblown leaf.
ISBN 0-15-200105-0
[1. Mice—Fiction. 2. Cats—Fiction. 3. Winds—Fiction.]
I. Schumaker, Ward, ill. II. Title.
PZ7.S24916Mo   1995
[E]—dc20   94-17010

First Edition

A B C D E

Printed in Singapore

The illustrations in this book are six-color hand-separated black-ink drawings.
The display type was set in Franklin Gothic Demi and Franklin Gothic Book
by Harcourt Brace & Company Photocomposition Center, San Diego, California.
The text type was set in Franklin Gothic Book by
Harcourt Brace & Company Photocomposition Center, San Diego, California.
Color separations by Bright Arts, Ltd., Singapore
Printed and bound by Tien Wah Press, Singapore
Production supervision by Warren Wallerstein and Kent MacElwee
Designed by Ward Schumaker and Lori J. McThomas

To Roger,
the wind beneath my wings.
With thanks to Sylvie for her
encouraging gusts.

—V. S.

For Matt, Debo, and Star,
the night Syl moved in.

—W. S.

Mouse creeps.

Cat purrs.

Cat sleeps.

Breeze rustles.

Cat stirs.

Mouse stops.

Cat s-t-r-e-t-c-h-e-s.

Whiskers twitch.

Mouse runs.

Cat chases.

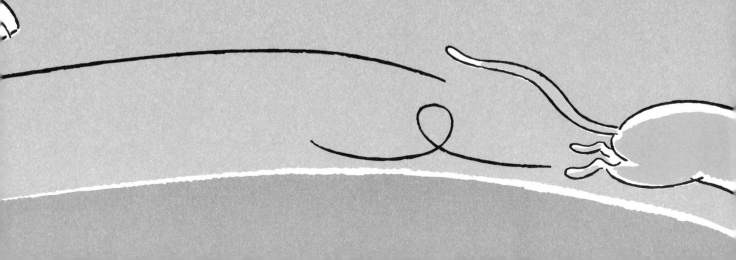

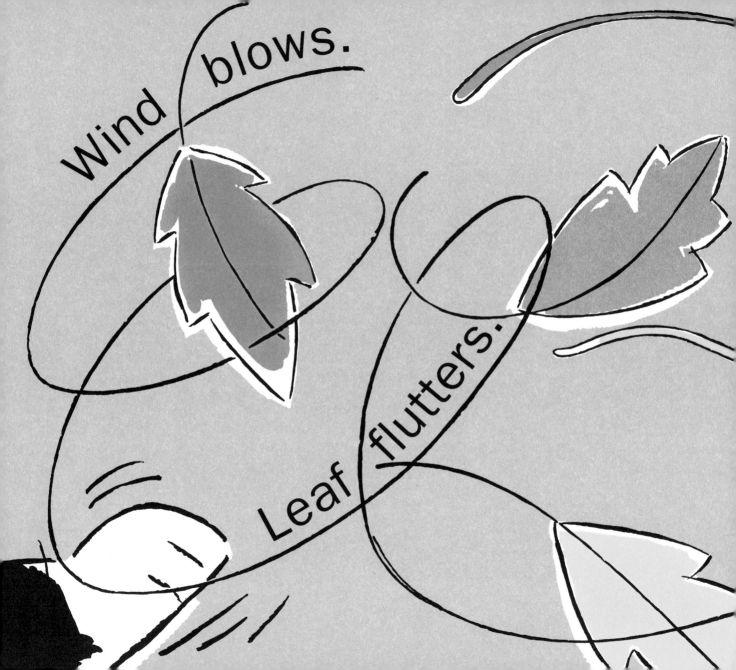

Mouse grabs.

Wind swirls.

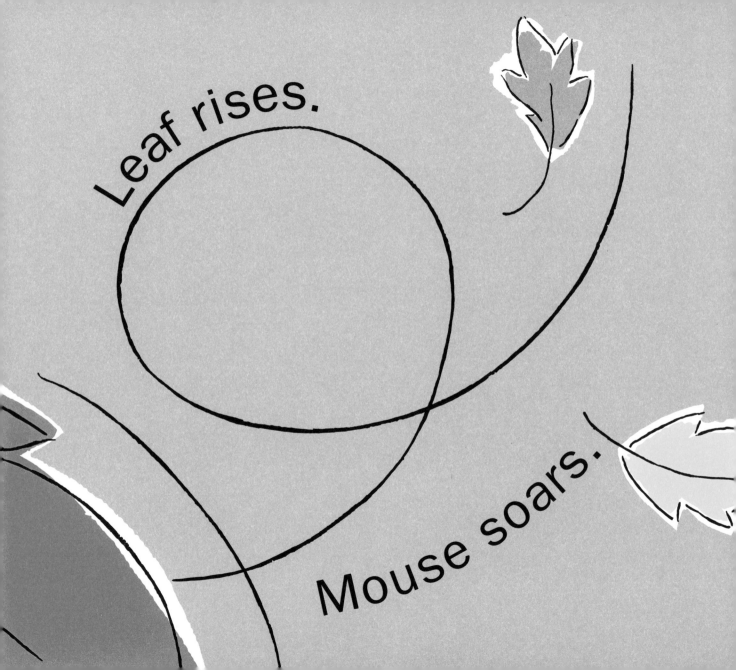

Leaf rises.

Mouse soars.

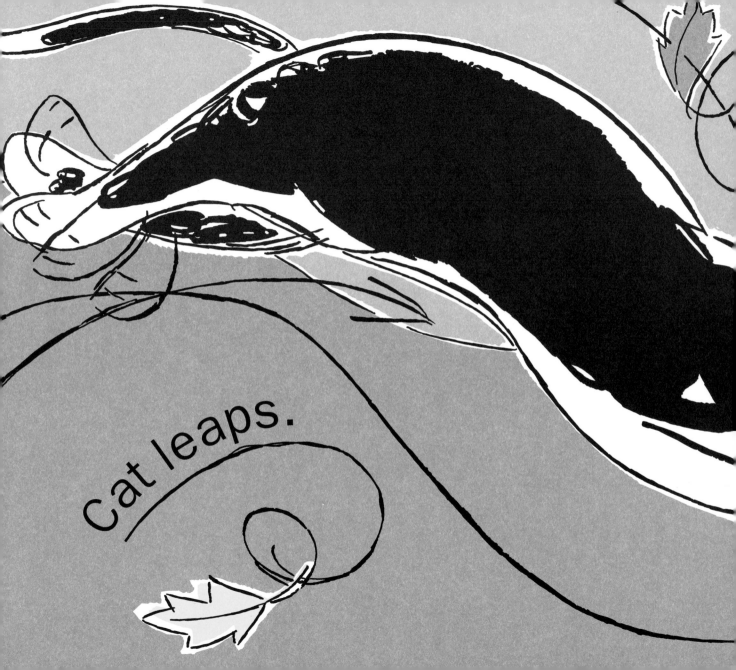

Cat leaps.

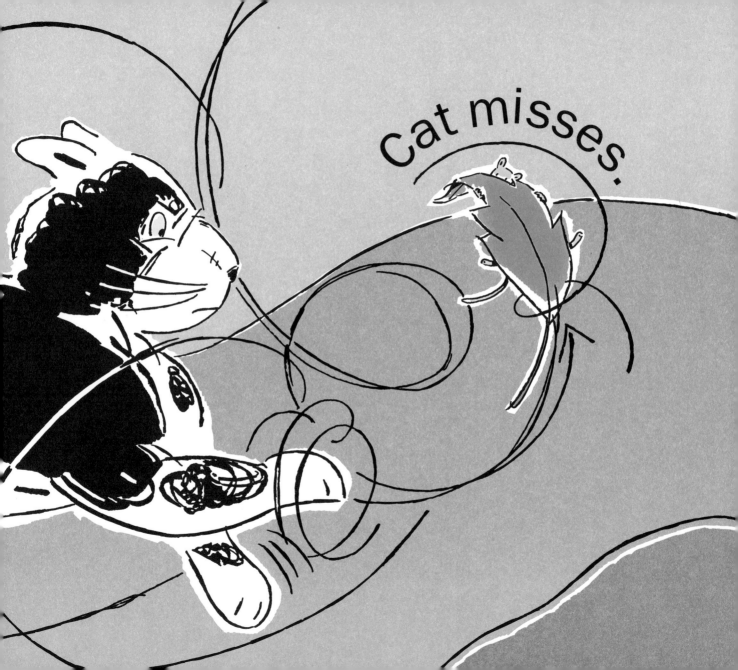

Wind whispers. Mouse glides.

Leaf dips.
Cat springs.

Cat splashes.

Leaf floats.

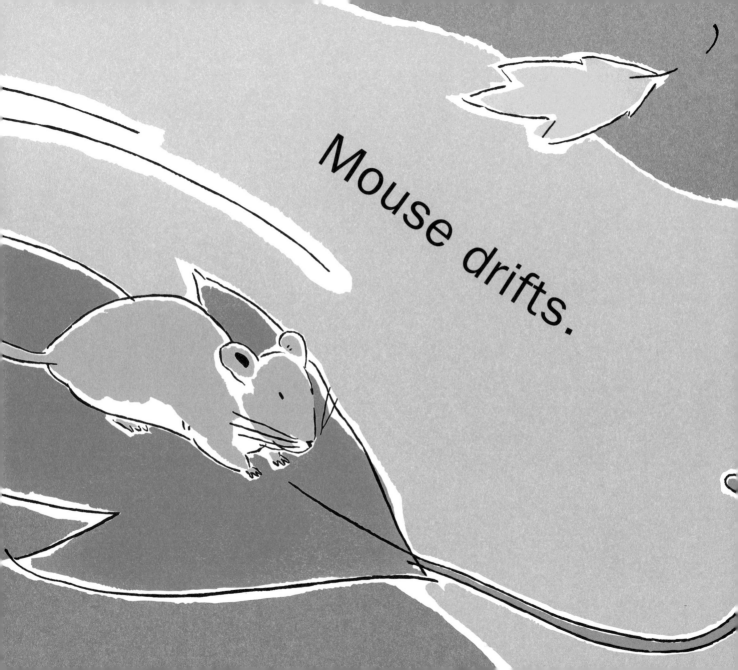

Mouse drifts.

Cat swats.

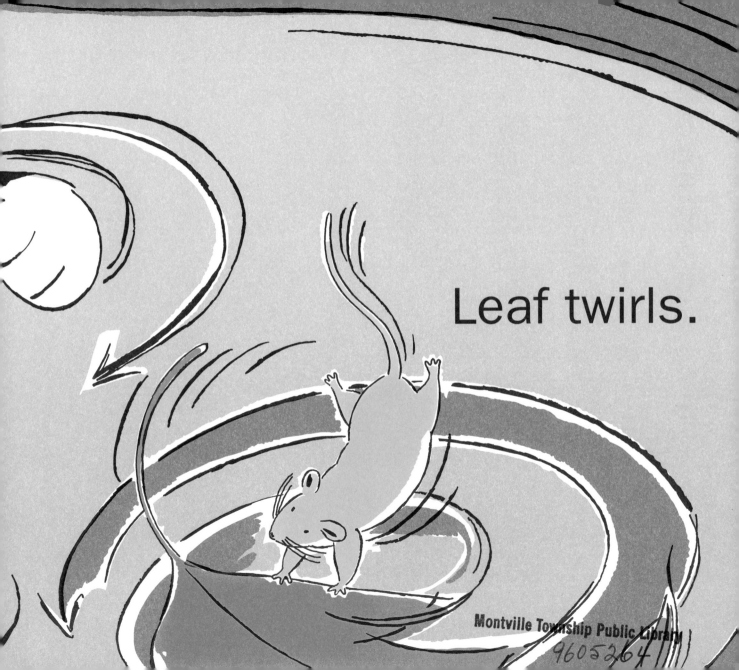

Leaf twirls.

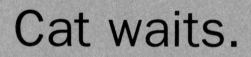

Cat waits.

Tail switches.

Wind howls.
Water swells.

Mouse sails.

Cat wails.

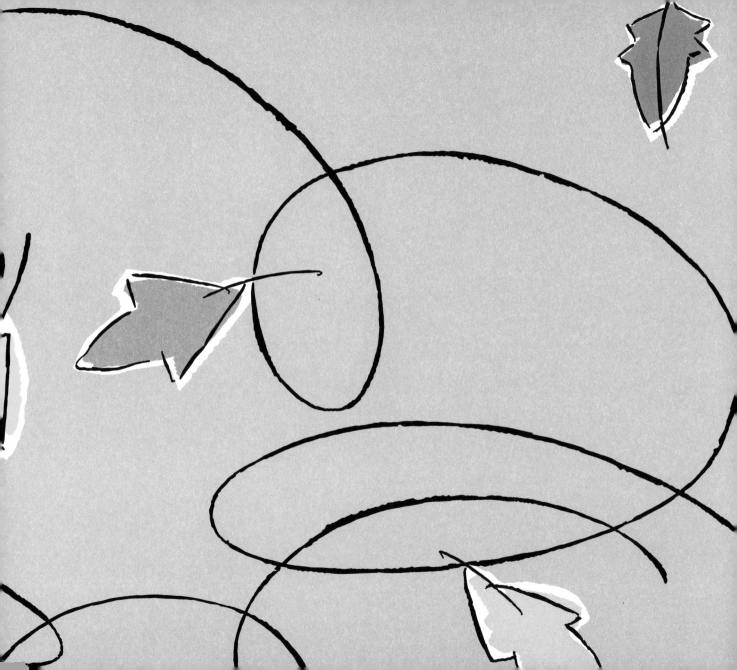